PUPPIES ON
PARADE

J
PB

Read all the books about Barkley's School for Dogs!

PUPPiES ON PARADE

By Marcia Thornton Jones and Debbie Dadey

Illustrated by Amy Wummer

Hyperion Books for Children
New York

To my mom, a terrific lady, Becky Gibson

—DD

To Helen Perelman, Emily Lo, and Amy Wummer:
a wagging good team, and that's the dog-honest
truth!

—MTJ

Printed in the United States of America
First Edition
1 3 5 7 9 10 8 6 4 2
Book design by Dawn Adelman
This book is set in 14-pt. Cheltenham.
ISBN 0-7868-1680-5
Visit www.barkleyschool.com

Contents

DUDLEY

I pulled. I tugged. I leapt. My pals and I were taking a field trip, and I knew exactly where we were going: the dog run. I couldn't wait, but Fred refused to move faster.

"Heel," Fred Barkley warned. I looked back at Fred's feet. Fred, the owner of Barkley's School for Dogs, was for some reason always talking about his feet. I figured it was because he only had two. Being a dog, I knew having only two feet was bound to slow down a human. Still, I thought he could be quicker.

"Why won't he hurry?" I whined to my pal Floyd.

Floyd was a beagle, and he liked fetching things. Anything. Today he carried a soggy tennis ball in his mouth, so it was a little hard to understand him.

"I think he wants us to practice walking on the leash," Floyd mumbled.

Blondie pranced beside Floyd. "We'll get there faster if we are patient," she told me. Blondie was the prettiest poodle to ever march down the sidewalks of our town. She was also one of my best friends.

Woodrow wasn't in a hurry to get to the dog run. Of course, Woodrow never hurried anywhere. I think it was because his short basset-hound legs just didn't go that fast. "Walk beside me," Woodrow suggested. "We'll get there soon enough."

As usual, Woodrow was right. As soon as I matched my long legs to Woodrow's

short ones, Fred Barkley grinned. He even scratched my ears and said, "Good dog." Of course, I knew this already. After all, I consider myself a Wonder Dog.

Finally, we got to the fence surrounding the dog run. The dog run at the park is perfect. For one thing, it has trees, bushes, and plenty of grass to sniff. But the best part is when Fred unsnaps our leashes and we can run, run, run.

As soon as I heard the click of my leash, I was off. As a Wonder Dog, I'm a pro at howling, scratching, catching tennis balls, and sneaking French fries off my human's plate. But I'm absolutely great at running. My floppy ears and bushy tail must have looked glorious flapping in the wind. I used my Wonder Dog speed to see how fast I could make my ears flap.

"Wait for me," Bubba yipped. Bubba was the youngest pup at Barkley's, and his puppy legs had to work three times as

hard to catch up to me. When he did, he tried to snatch my tail in his puppy mouth. That's just like a puppy.

My other friends bounded after us. Floyd even let us share his tennis ball. We were having a great time, especially since Sweetcakes—Barkley's very own bully dog—was keeping her nose out of our business for a change.

I won't say Sweetcakes is mean, but one thing is a Fido Fact. Sweetcakes definitely isn't nice. In fact, if I had to choose between spending a day with Sweetcakes or inviting a family of fleas to live on my tail, I'm sure I would pick the fleas.

The fact that Sweetcakes was nowhere around bothered me. I wondered if she was planning to attack us when we least expected it. I was so busy looking for Sweetcakes I almost ran over a pug dog.

"I'm sorry," I told the little guy. "I didn't see you."

The pug shook dust from his tail and tilted his head. "I am not at all bothered," he said. "My name is Dudley, by the way."

I grinned down at the new dog and nodded. "My name's Jack, and I go to Barkley's School for Dogs."

"Pleased to make your acquaintance," he said.

Dudley talked with long words. I lifted my ears a bit, but that didn't help me understand him. "Huh?" I said.

"I'm happy to meet you," Dudley explained. "I'm here with the rest of my friends from Howl's Dog City."

I backed away from Dudley. "Howl's Dog City?" I said. Okay, let me be honest. I had heard about Howl's. What dog hadn't? It's uptown and full of dogs that think they rule the streets. "Did you say Howl's?"

Dudley blinked his big round eyes. "Why, yes indeed. I go to Howl's. It is quite nice."

If Dudley was from Howl's, then I knew trouble was just around the corner. I had heard plenty about the dogs at that school. It was up to me, Jack the Wonder Dog, to warn my friends.

2

SPUNKY

"Blondie! Woodrow! Floyd! Bubba!" I barked as I dashed away from Dudley. I left that Howl's dog standing in my dust, blinking his big round eyes.

Blondie, Woodrow, and Floyd sniffed my nose when I finally caught up to them. Bubba hopped up and down in front of me. "What is it? What is it?" Bubba yipped.

Once I had caught my breath, I told my friends the bad news. "The dogs from Howl's Dog City are here."

Blondie gasped. Floyd dropped his tennis ball. Bubba stopped hopping and looked at me with a tilted head. "What's Howl's Dog City?" Bubba asked.

"It's just the most stuck-up school for dogs, in town," Blondie answered for me.

Floyd nodded. "The dogs at Howl's think they're better than anyone. They're mean and selfish. I heard they wouldn't even think of sharing their toys." Floyd scooped up his tennis ball and chewed on it.

"Now, wait just a doggone minute," Woodrow said. "It's not a good idea to believe everything you hear. Those could be rumors and nothing more."

Bubba scratched his ear, his puppy eyes thoughtful. "What's a rumor?"

"Rumors are stories that are told from one pooch to another," Blondie explained. "Sometimes they're true. Other times they aren't."

I stepped up and added with true Wonder Dog wisdom, "I'm willing to bet my tail that the Howl's stories are the dog-honest truth," I said.

"Hang on to your tail," Woodrow said with a grin, "because here come some of the Howl's dogs right now."

A German shepherd with pointy ears and a slender muzzle zeroed in on us. This was not your normal hi-I'm-glad-to-see-you kind of dog. This was more your I'm-going-to-eat-you-up-and-spit-you-out kind of dog. Dudley trotted next to him.

Needless to say, I smelled trouble. This German shepherd looked like the meanest dog I had ever met—even meaner than Sweetcakes.

I must admit, I was ready to turn tail and run. Of course, that was impossible because Bubba was in my way, huddling behind me.

The German shepherd stopped right in front of us. The sun glinted in his black eyes, and he licked his chops as if he were ready to gobble us up in one bite.

"Dudley here tells me you dogs are from Barkley's," the German shepherd said. His voice was low and growly. "My name is Spunky."

I tried to remember my name, but with a dog the size of Spunky glaring at me, it was impossible. Not for Woodrow. He stepped toward Spunky as if he were just another dog.

"I'm Woodrow," my friend said. "This is Blondie, Floyd, Bubba, and Jack."

Spunky turned his attention on Woodrow. "You must be the leader of the pack."

Woodrow didn't have a chance to answer. Just then, Barkley's very own Sweetcakes trotted up. Clyde, the bull-dog, followed her.

"I'm the one and only leader around here," Sweetcakes snarled.

"Yeah. Yeah, leader," Clyde repeated. He followed Sweetcakes everywhere and had a habit of agreeing with anything she said.

Seeing Sweetcakes and Spunky nose to nose was enough to cause doggie nightmares. Fortunately, before any fur flew, Fred Barkley and the man who must have been the owner of Howl's walked over, leashes in hand.

"The parade will be the biggest thing this town has seen," Fred was saying.

"It's not every year we celebrate our hundredth anniversary," said Howl's owner. "I'm glad we get to be a part of it."

My ears perked up. Parade? That sounded like fun, and I wanted to hear more.

Spunky puffed up his chest and grinned at us, spoiling everything. "Did you hear that? I'll be leading the parade for Howl's Dog City," he bragged.

Before I could hear any more, a familiar fuzzy shape sashayed across the dog run.

Tazz. I was used to the black-and-gold cat. She lived in my apartment building and had the nerve to show up in dog territory. Like now.

"I know a thing or two about parades," Tazz told us. She taunted Spunky by parading right past him.

Spunky eyed Tazz as if she were a T-bone steak. Then he sped across the

dog run, barking a war cry. Howl's dogs came from every corner.

Tazz eyed Spunky and his gang. She twitched her bushy tail and waited until the dogs were closing in on her. Then, she burst into action. Tazz dashed across the ground and flew up a tree, just out of Spunky's reach.

Spunky jumped. Spunky snapped his teeth at Tazz's tail. Spunky growled. His huge teeth gleamed in the sunlight.

I realized then and there that I was one lucky hound. I was lucky that Spunky didn't go to Barkley's School for Dogs. I trembled at the thought of both Sweetcakes and Spunky terrorizing Barkley's School for Dogs together.

It would be like King Kong and Godzilla ruling the play yard.

LEADER OF
THE PACK

The next morning, Maggie came down-stairs jingling my leash.

"Let's go, Jack. I'm visiting your school today. I have the day off," she said. Now normally, I'd be thrilled to have Maggie at my school. I loved being around my human, but if she didn't have to go to her school, then why did I have to go to mine? I mean, fair is fair.

Oh, well, life is not always fair for a dog. I've found that out many times. Besides, having Maggie at my school could make

17

for an exciting day. When we got to Barkley's I held my head high in the air. I was proud to have Maggie there, and I told my friends about it.

"Maggie's here to play with me," I bragged to Floyd.

Floyd looked up from his rubber reindeer and shook his head. "I think Maggie is here to do something else."

Something else? What could be more important than playing with me? I trotted over to see what Maggie was up to. I came nose to nose with purple paint.

"Stay back, Jack," Maggie told me gently. "You'll smear the paint."

What was this? I stood back and watched. Fred and Maggie were so busy painting letters on a long banner, they didn't even notice me sitting behind them. I tried to figure out what they were writing, but the letters made no sense. I knew just the friend for this job.

Woodrow was the only dog that could read. It wasn't easy nudging him up from his nap, but I did it.

When Maggie and Fred went inside, Woodrow sniffed the sign. He turned his head one way, then another. Lots of dogs gathered around to see what he was up to.

Finally, Woodrow cleared his throat and announced, "This is a sign for the parade. It says 'Puppies on Parade.'"

"That's the parade the dogs from

Howl's were bragging about," I told my pals.

"A parade!" Blondie giggled. "I've always wanted to be in a parade."

Bubba danced around and sang, "Parade. Parade. I'm going to be in a parade."

"It'll be dog-awesome!" I yipped. "I'll be the grand pup leading all the other dogs." I figured it was only right that I lead. After all, I am a Wonder Dog.

Floyd lifted his head from his chew toy.

"Maybe I could lead the parade," he suggested.

That's when about six other dogs started whining that they could be the leaders. Sweetcakes put a growling stop to the argument. She barked, and everyone listened. "You mutts may not even make it to the parade. Fred will want only the best dog there to show off his school. And I am the best dog."

Boss

I was mad. I had just as much right to be the head dog in the parade as Sweetcakes did. I sat under a big oak tree and frowned so hard I felt my forehead wrinkle. If you've ever seen a dog frowning, then you know it isn't pretty.

I'll tell you something else that isn't pretty. Tazz. She loves to pester me. "Hi, Blunder Dog," Tazz purred from the top of the wall that surrounds Barkley's.

I turned my back to Tazz and kept

frowning. "What's got your fur all in a bunch?" Tazz asked.

I didn't really want to tell Tazz, but everything just came out. I blabbed about how I wanted to be the leader of the parade.

"That's the craziest thing I've ever heard," Tazz said. "Why would anyone want to lead a bunch of dogs in straight lines? Cats are smarter than that."

"Spunky is going to be in the parade," I told Tazz. I figured Tazz hadn't forgotten being chased by Spunky.

Tazz hissed. I must admit a cat hissing is downright doggie-bone chilling. "I wouldn't want to be anywhere near that brute," she said. "Besides, I already know I'm the grandest thing on four legs. I don't need a parade for that."

I didn't need a parade either. After all, I was a Wonder Dog. But I *wanted* a parade. I wanted to make Maggie proud by being the leader. I could just imagine walking at the head of the Barkley pack. I sighed and looked up at the wall.

Tazz licked a paw and laughed. "You do know that all of Howl's is going to be in the parade. Don't you?"

I hadn't known that, but I wasn't about to let Tazz know, so I fibbed just a bit. "Of course I know." I looked down at my nose to make sure it wasn't growing like a storybook character's. Whenever Pinocchio told a lie, his nose grew. Thankfully, my snout stayed the same.

Tazz stood up straight and stretched. "Did you know that the dogs at Howl's plan to show everyone that they're better than Barkley's?"

I think everyone would agree that I'm a friendly kind of dog. But when I thought about the dogs at Howl's wanting to beat us, I have to admit I felt a growl work its way up from my chest. The dogs at Howl's were terrible. The Barkley dogs would have to show them who was boss, and I knew just how to do it.

THE ABSOLUTE WORST

I couldn't do it alone. I needed help. I knew I could depend on my friends. I sniffed out Floyd, Blondie, and Woodrow. Bubba, being a curious pup, hopped between us where we huddled near the brick wall. A few other dogs wandered over to see what I had to say. I chose my words carefully.

"The dogs from Howl's are the absolute worst," I said. That made every ear perk up. Even Woodrow's droopy ears lifted a full inch off the ground.

Blondie nodded. "An old boxer that lives in my apartment building said that he met a spaniel from Howl's. Do you know what that Howl's dog did? He stole the boxer's ball right from his mouth. It's the dog-honest truth!"

Floyd gripped his chew toy a little more firmly between his teeth.

"That's nothing," Casanova said. The little Chihuahua's eyes were round and troubled. "I heard that the dogs from Howl's won't let anything smaller than a Rottweiler play in their school yard. They *sit* on the smaller dogs and use them as pillows."

A little terrier named Petey stopped digging a hole, long enough to nod. "They're bullies, all right. Everyone knows it. I heard they won't let best friends speak to each other!"

Scarlett and Rhett, two Irish setters, moved closer together and whimpered.

Tails slumped to the ground and a few dogs let out worried whines. It seemed like every dog at Barkley's had a bad story about Howl's. Everybody, that is, except Woodrow. He slowly shook his head, his droopy ears making tracks in the grass. "I never believe what I hear," Woodrow said, his voice slow and serious, "without finding out for myself."

I stepped to the front of the pack and spoke with true Wonder Dog wisdom.

After all, I knew something they didn't know. "We can believe what we hear about Howl's," I told Woodrow and everyone else. "I know for a fact that the hounds from Howl's are planning to take over the parade just so they can prove they're better than us."

"How terrible," Blondie gasped.

"And mean," Bubba said with a puppy whine.

"They'll ruin the parade for everyone,"

Casanova yipped. "And I bet they'll try to sit on me!"

I interrupted with a short bark. "They won't," I said, "as long as we do something about it, and I have the perfect plan. But I need your help."

"Name it," Petey said, "and we'll do it."

All the other dogs nodded. Everyone, of course, except Woodrow. He waited to hear what I had to say first.

"I'll be the leader of our marching

pack," I announced, "and we'll practice together before the big day. Follow me, and we'll show those dogs from Howl's who the best pups in the parade really are!"

"It'll be dog-awesome," Floyd said. He was so excited he didn't even notice he had dropped his chew toy.

Blondie batted her eyelashes. "I'll get my hair brushed until it floats like a cloud," she said. "It will be truly beautiful."

Even Woodrow stood up a little taller.

Then he slumped back down. "Maybe we shouldn't be turning this parade into a competition," he told his friends.

"We have to," Rhett said.

"Those uptown hounds from Howl's are planning to wipe our noses in the dust," Scarlett told him.

"But what about Sweetcakes?" Floyd asked.

I gulped and shook my head. We had to forget about Sweetcakes for now. "We *have* to show Howl's that Barkley's dogs are better," I said. "It's up to us!"

PUPPY PANIC

Don't get me wrong. If I had a choice, I would just lie around the apartment with Maggie, letting her scratch my ears. But since that wasn't to be, I could hardly wait to get to school the next day. We had work to do.

Maggie was excited, too. I could tell, because she didn't mind one bit that I was tugging on the leash to get to Barkley's School for Dogs. As soon as we arrived, Maggie rushed over to the long banner hanging on the wall. More words filled the sign. I gave it a passing sniff.

A few other dogs were clustered in the main office, waiting for Fred to let them out to play. "What else do you think that banner says?" Bubba asked me.

"I can't tell for sure," I told him. "But I hope it says 'Barkley's is the best: better than all the rest, and especially better than those uptown snobs from Howl's.'"

Bubba cocked his head to look at the

banner. "That would be an awfully long sign, but it should say that," he agreed.

The bells over the door jingled, and Woodrow plodded into the office with his human. Before we had time to say hello, Fred clapped his hands.

"Great," Fred said. "We're all here early. We can go ahead and have our lesson!"

I sighed. Going to school wasn't so bad, since all my friends were here. But school would've been a lot better if Fred didn't insist on trying to teach us. I definitely didn't have time for Fred's lessons today. There was only one thing to do. I would have to hurry Fred through all the learning stuff.

As soon as we were outside, Fred pulled out a short leash. Very short. "Today we'll practice walking on the leash," he said. "Nicely." He pointed straight at me when he said that last part.

My tail drooped and my ears flopped.

Walking on a leash is my least favorite thing to do. But I knew the secret to good leash walking.

"Go fast," I whispered to the dog next to me. "Pass it on." I wanted to help everyone be their best.

I heard my suggestion being whispered into one floppy ear after another. As I said, my friends never let me down. As soon as Fred snapped the leash onto their collars, they trotted so fast Fred had to hurry. When it was my turn, I tore across the lawn, tugging and pulling at the leash to make sure Fred was behind me.

"Slow down," Fred said, giving the leash a gentle tug. Then he started talking about his feet again.

"Heel," he said. "HEEL."

Even though I was in a hurry, I was

nice. I looked back at Fred's feet, just the way he wanted. But I didn't stop. I kept running. *Bam!* I ran right into a tree. Let me tell you, running into a tree can hurt!

Fred kneeled down and scratched my ears. "Jack," he said, "you have too much energy. In fact, all you dogs do. What you need is exercise. How about a trip to the dog run?"

I couldn't believe my Wonder Dog ears. We were going to my favorite place! This was perfect. We could plan our puppy parade there!

As soon as we reached the run, I gathered my friends close.

"We have to plan the parade," I told them. "Now, what should we do?"

I looked at my friends. Floyd chewed on a rubber ball. Blondie batted her eyelashes. Woodrow scratched an ear while Bubba tried to bite the white tip on the basset's tail. No one had a single idea.

"To be honest," Rhett said, "I've never *been* to a parade."

"Me neither," said Petey. "What do humans actually do at one?"

All my friends started talking at once. I put down my paw and quieted the group with a quick yip. "It's obvious," I said, "that a parade is the time to show what we do best."

The rest of the dogs thought about this for a full fifteen seconds. Then their tails started wagging.

"I like to fetch," Floyd said.

"I can dig holes," Petey said. There was a dried clump of dirt on his nose as proof.

Bubba hopped up and down. "I like to chase my tail—and other tails, too."

"I'm pretty good at jumping," Blondie said in a shy voice.

Scarlett and Rhett pushed to the front of the group. "We can run in zigzags better than any other dog around."

"I can yap," Casanova yapped, proving his point.

Of course, I was known for my wondrous howling. I didn't say it because everyone already knew it as a Fido Fact.

"Then that's what we'll do," I said. "We'll prove we're the best by doing what we're good at."

"Are you sure that's such a good idea?" Woodrow asked. "Maybe we should think about it some more."

"We're done thinking," I decided. "It's time to show everyone in town we're the best. Are you ready to practice?"

Everyone nodded. Everybody except Woodrow.

"Go!" I howled.

I kept howling. Scarlett and Rhett ran in zigzags. Unfortunately, when they did, they ran right over Petey, who was trying to dig a hole. Petey stumbled backward and knocked over Floyd, who was busy

throwing his ball in the air. Blondie tried to jump over Floyd, but Bubba was chasing her tail, and she tripped.

Woodrow, I am sorry to say, watched us with a crooked grin on his face. "You are definitely the best at one thing," he said once we'd all landed in a pile. "Causing puppy panic!"

FUNNY-LOOKING

"The only pack you're leading is a pack of clowns," Sweetcakes told me with a snicker.

"Yeah, yeah," Clyde panted. "Clowns."

I was ready to give Sweetcakes and Clyde a big piece of my mind, but I was interrupted by a loud noise. It was Spunky, from Howl's. He wasn't alone. All the dogs from Howl's stared at us and laughed.

I guess we must have made a funny sight, sprawled all over the ground. But I

didn't care. It made me boiling mad that the Howl's dogs were laughing.

"Come on," Blondie said, sticking her white nose up in the air. "Let's go where there are nice dogs."

All the dogs from Barkley's huddled together on one side of the dog run. The dogs from Howl's stood on the other side. "We can't let those Howl's dogs ruin everything," Floyd said.

"We have to stick together," I told my

friends. I had to convince everyone.

To my surprise, I saw Sweetcakes nodding. Sweetcakes actually agreed with me. I hardly knew what to say next. After all, Sweetcakes had never agreed with me about anything.

"I've had it with that rotten Spunkarella dog," Sweetcakes said, loud enough for all the dogs in the run to hear.

"Yeah, yeah," Clyde panted loudly. "Spunkarella."

The hair stood up on Spunky's neck and he showed his teeth to Sweetcakes. Every dog knows that showing your teeth to another dog is a challenge to fight. Every dog, except for Sweetcakes and Spunky, took one step back.

Things were definitely getting out of hand. I, Jack the Wonder Dog, had to do something. But what?

Dudley, the little dog from Howl's, appeared at my side. "We have to stop them," Dudley told me. I agreed, but I didn't tell Dudley that.

"You guys shouldn't have laughed at us," I snapped at Dudley.

Dudley shrugged his shoulders. "Sorry about that, but you must admit you were all a bit funny-looking."

"We aren't funny," I snapped at Dudley. "In fact, since you've been coming to the dog run, we haven't had any fun at all."

Dudley's little ears perked up. "Sorry to hear that, but I don't see that it's our fault."

I opened my mouth to speak, but a growl stopped me. It was Sweetcakes. She was getting closer and closer to Spunky.

B FOR BARKLEY'S

Maybe you've seen old movies where someone saves the day at the last minute. That's what happened at the dog run. Fred snapped a leash on Sweetcakes and led us all home. Fred saved the day. Humans do that every once in a while.

Blondie stuck her nose up in the air and complained all the way home. "I don't think those Howl's dogs are very nice. They shouldn't laugh at us."

I nodded. Sure Sweetcakes had laughed at us, but we were used to that.

"Spunky wasn't scared of Sweetcakes," Floyd pointed out. "That took a lot of guts."

I had to admit that Spunky wasn't a scaredy-cat. He had a lot of spunk. Either that, or he was crazy.

I forgot about Spunky when we got back to Barkley's. Maggie was waiting for us beside a huge box in the front office. Maggie and Fred opened the box as we tried to guess what was inside.

"What could it be?" Bubba asked. "Bones?"

"Chew toys?" Floyd asked hopefully.

Woodrow lifted his long snout. "Prime rib sounds good to me."

I couldn't help wondering, myself. I loved surprises that came in boxes. Maybe the box was full of canned dog food. That stuff was dog-awesome.

"It's full of sweaters!" Blondie said as Maggie pulled out a bright green sweater.

A big groan came from a few of the dogs. Sweaters were definitely not as good as canned dog food or chew bones.

"Those are so cute," Blondie said. "That color will look great against my white hair."

I had to admit they were growl-ariffic. After all, if Maggie had brought them, they had to be good. Each sweater had a giant B stitched on them.

"That *B* stands for *Barkley's*," Woodrow told us.

"I wish they were blue," Bubba said. "I like blue."

"Why didn't they put our name on the sweaters?" Scarlett complained.

"They could have put *Barkley's* instead of just a *B*," Rhett said.

"Stripes would have been pretty too," Harry the Westie said. "I have a striped bed at home."

It seemed everyone had something to say about the sweaters, even after we got outside in the play yard. Complaints were jumping around like fleas in a frying pan.

Bubba whined. "This is no fun. I just want to march in the parade."

I was getting pretty tired of all the fussing myself. Things got even worse when more trouble showed up: trouble with a capital T.

TEAM

Trouble was named Tazz. She stood on the top of the wall and swished her long tail back and forth like a whip.

"Dogs in sweaters?" she meowed. "It's enough to give me catnap nightmares. Between you and those horrible hounds from Howl's, I may not sleep for a week."

I didn't believe her for a split second. After all, she was already yawning.

Petey hopped up, trying to reach Tazz. "What does a cat know about Howl's?" he asked.

Tazz settled down on top of the wall, wrapping her bushy tail around her paws. She took her time answering, using a paw to wipe her whiskers first.

Finally, she blinked those big yellow eyes and looked back at us. "A cat knows all," she said with a smirk. "And I know that the dogs at Howl's are planning to wear sweaters, too."

"They must have stolen Fred's idea," Blondie said with a huff.

Tazz stood up and arched her back in a stretch. "They will look like a real team when they show up at the parade wearing those matching sweaters," she said.

"We're the better team," I howled at her.

Tazz blinked her amber eyes three times. "You don't look like a team to me," she meowed. Then she jumped off the wall.

My pals sat still for a full three seconds. Then Floyd dropped the rubber ball he had been chewing. "Are we a team or not?" he asked.

"Of course we're a team," Scarlett said.

"We have to be a team," Rhett added.

"Barkley's is the best team in town," I added with Wonder Dog conviction.

Bubba scratched an ear. "What *is* a team?" he asked.

Bubba sat there, head cocked, looking up at me. So did the rest of the dogs. We never really thought about it before.

"Well," I said slowly. "Teams have something to do with winning."

"My human is on a team," Floyd said. "They run up and down a field chasing a ball. A team must have something to do with chasing balls."

Rhett and Scarlett shook their heads. "That can't be," Scarlett said. "We know two horses that pull a carriage around

the park. They're a team, and it has nothing to do with a ball. A team must have something to do with pulling."

Then it seemed like everybody was talking at once.

Suddenly, I sat down on my tail and watched everyone argue. This didn't feel like a team at all.

"Guys," I said softly. "Hey, guys," I said a little louder.

Nobody heard me, they were too busy yapping. There was only one thing for me to do. I pointed my nose to the highest branch of a nearby tree and let loose with a Wonder Dog howl.

I don't mean to brag, but my howl is so loud, it's been known to bring speeding buses to a screeching halt. It definitely got my buddies' attention.

"We've got it all wrong. A team is a group working together to get something done," I said.

"Like ants?" Bubba asked. "They work together."

"Exactly," I said with a grin. "We haven't been a team because we haven't worked together."

For the first time since I've known him, Woodrow actually got excited. He hopped up on his stubby legs and his tail wagged so fast it became a blur. "Jack is right," Woodrow said. "We've been going about this parade all wrong. What we have to do

is work as a team, and to do that we have to do two things. Work together and have fun."

Bubba's ears perked up. "Did you say fun? I like the sound of that!"

"Can you tell us how to be a team?" Casanova asked. "What do we have to do to prove Barkley's is the best?"

Woodrow shook his head. "It's not about being best. It's about showing what Barkley's is all about."

"That's easy," Floyd said. "Barkley's is about dogs."

"I think it's about playing," Bubba yipped.

"And friends," Blondie said. I was sure she winked at me when she said it, too.

"Don't forget about the tricks Fred teaches us," Casanova added.

"That's right," Woodrow said. "This parade is supposed to be a celebration."

"So let's celebrate!" I cheered.

PUPPiES ON PARADE

I couldn't wait. Maggie was taking forever to put on her sneakers. I'm glad I never have to put anything on my feet.

Finally, she snapped on my leash and I pulled her down the steps of our apartment building to the sidewalk. I didn't stop to sniff a single tree, bush, or telephone pole. I was in a hurry. This was the big day.

The park was bustling with activity. People milled around, getting floats ready. Several groups stood around tooting on horns and flutes. Being a dog, I didn't need an instrument to make noise. I lifted my nose and barked, trying to find my friends. A familiar voice answered. I pulled Maggie toward the dogs clustered inside the dog run.

"I'm ready to show Howl's our best celebration," I panted when I reached my buddies. We were a handsome bunch, all of us wearing the bright green sweater with the giant *B* on them. I must admit,

the feel of the sweater on my back made me prance a little more than usual.

I glanced across the dog run to where the dogs from Howl's stood. They wore the same sweaters, too, but with the letter *H*. The thought of it made me want to snag that smug pug Dudley's sweater with my eyetooth and give it a tug.

Maggie left me with the other dogs while she helped Fred unroll the banner they had made.

"What's it say?" Bubba asked.

Woodrow sat down and stared long and hard at the banner. Finally, he looked at us. "It says," he said slowly, "what it said before. 'Puppies on Parade!'"

"What's that line underneath say?" Blondie asked. "That part wasn't there before."

"It says," Woodrow told us all, "'Barkley's School for Dogs and Howl's Dog City.'"

"You mean, we're marching *with* Howl's?" Sweetcakes whimpered.

"That's exactly what it means," Woodrow said. We all stared across the dog run at the Howl's hounds.

Spunky grinned and trotted right toward me. The rest of the Howl's dogs followed.

"Marching together!" Spunky said. "What a wagging-good idea!"

This didn't make any sense to me. After

all, Spunky was mean. Wasn't he? "You mean, you *want* to be in the parade together?" I asked. "With us? The dogs from Barkley's?"

Spunky's tail swished back and forth and he nodded. "Of course. Why wouldn't we? We thought *you* didn't like *us*!"

Suddenly, I remembered what Woodrow had told us. Never believe what you hear without finding out for yourself. I realized Woodrow was right. I had believed all the stories about the Howl's dogs. But that's all they were—stories. Not a single one was true.

I took a step toward Spunky and took a deep Wonder Dog breath. "We owe you an apology," I said. "We were wrong. Dog-wrong."

"In fact," Blondie said as she joined me. "We were mean."

"And rude," Bubba added in his puppy voice. "And we're sorry."

All the Barkley's dogs agreed. All but one, that is. Sweetcakes pushed her way to the front of the pack. She stood, nose to nose, with Spunky. "I'm not apologizing," she said with a snarl. "I never apologize."

The rest of us held our breaths. I expected hair to fly, but I was wrong.

Sweetcakes took a step back and glanced at the banner. "No, I won't apologize," she repeated, "but I won't mind

if your group marches with Barkley's."

Spunky cocked his head to look at Sweetcakes. "Then I believe it's a truce," he said, "between you and me."

Tails suddenly started wagging so hard they caused a breeze.

That's how Fred and the Howl's Dog City owner found us when they came to line us up for the big parade. I ended up right next to Dudley the pug.

"I'm sorry," I told Dudley. "I hope you'll give the Barkley dogs another chance. We're really quite a friendly pack."

"Why, of course. I knew all along you were an upstanding canine."

I didn't have the slightest idea what Dudley meant, but I smiled at him anyway. I had a feeling it meant he liked me, and I was glad.

I held up my head and marched out into the park, side by side with my new pals from Howl's. This time we celebrated

as a real team—one that got along. It was silly to believe all those rumors about Howl's when they were actually a pack of friendly pups. Making new friends is dog-awesome!